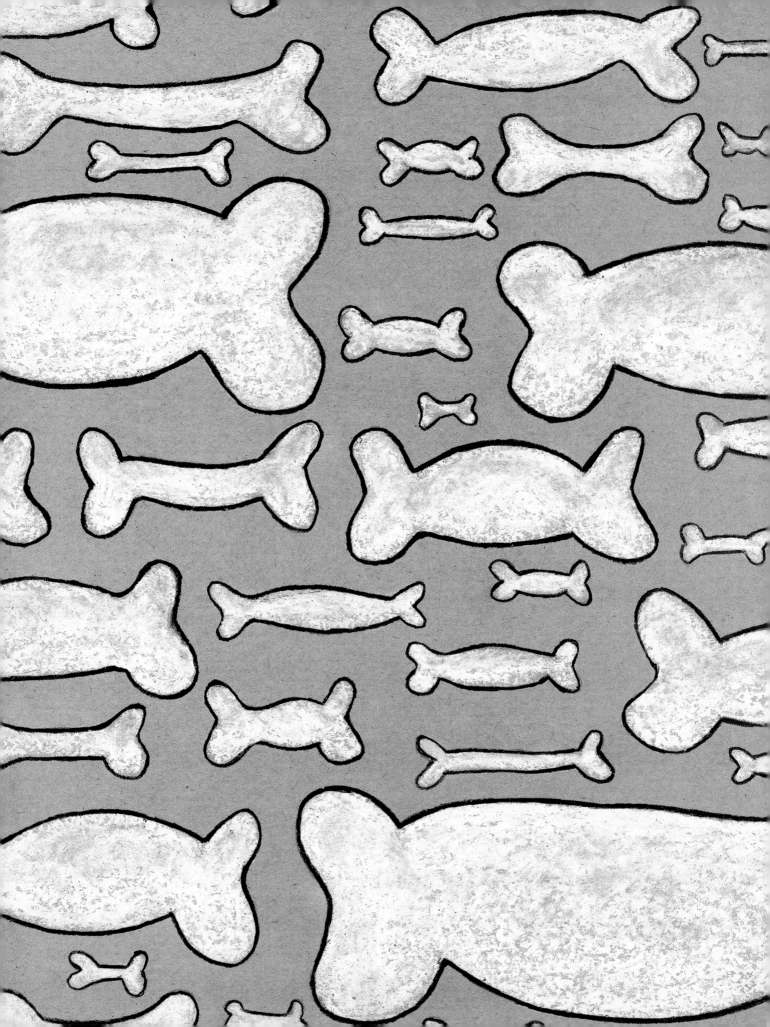

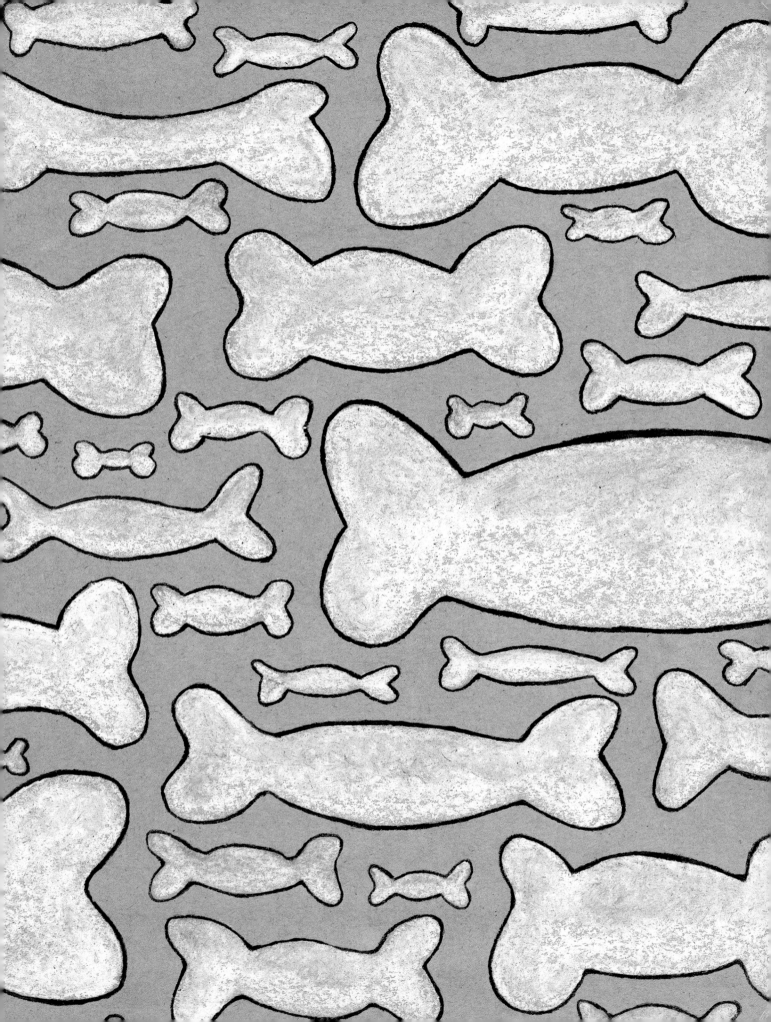

A Dog Needs a Bone!

A Dog Needs a Bone!

STORY AND PICTURES BY

Audrey Wood

THE BLUE SKY PRESS

An Imprint of Scholastic Inc. • New York

This book was originally published by the Blue Sky Press in 2007.

ISBN-13: 978-0-545-09913-4
ISBN-10: 0-545-09913-7

12 11 10 9 8 7 6 5 4 3 2 1   8 9 10 11 12 13/0

Printed in the U.S.A.   66

This edition first printing, September 2008

For my dog friends:

Sumo, Duffy, Zara, Lily, Enzo,

Nona, Mandrake, Twilight,

Happy, Sheba, Freddie,

and Little Dog.

And for my cat friends, too:

Gizmo, George, and

Roona Roo.

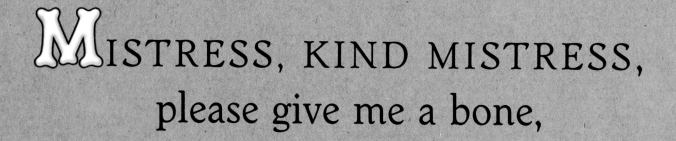

MISTRESS, KIND MISTRESS,
please give me a bone,

and I'll stay by your side,
no more will I roam.

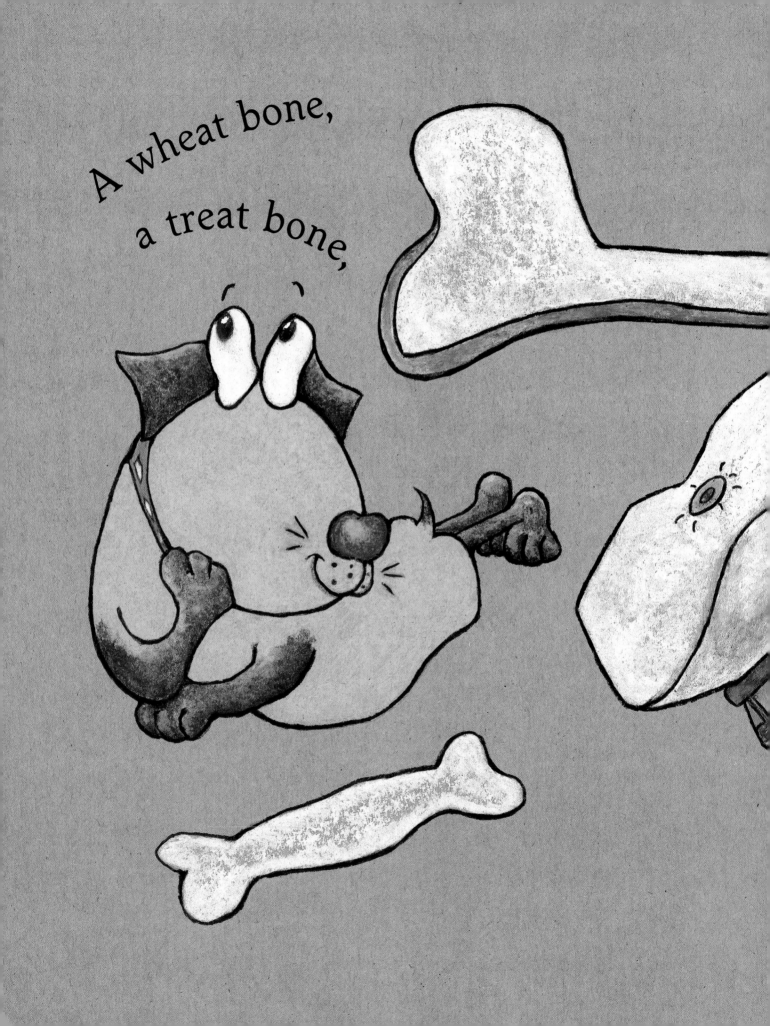

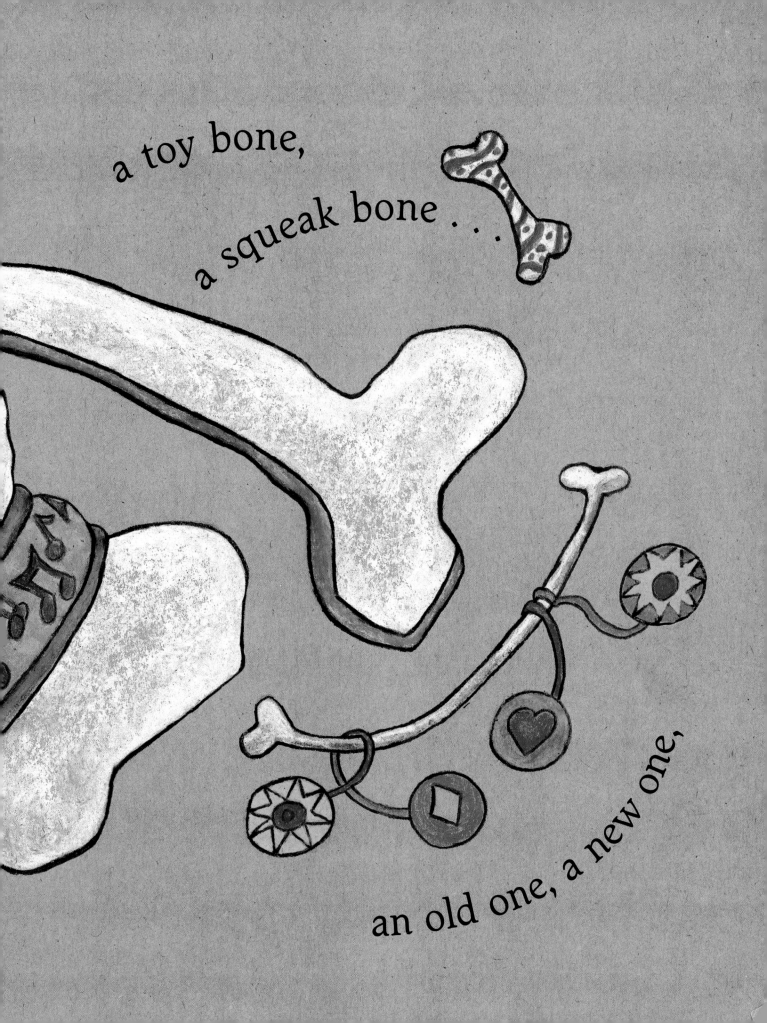

I simply must have
something to chew on!

Will my mistress
PLEASE give me a bone?

I'll sweep your floors.

I'll answer your phone.

I'll treat you like a queen on a throne.

I'll never chase cats,

or howl at the moon,

or play with the paper
in your pink powder room.

If my mistress will
PLEASE
give me a bone!

OH, NO!
Where did she go?

My mistress has left me.
I'm sad and alone.

What will I do
when she is not home?

I KNOW . . .

I'll snuggle the scarf

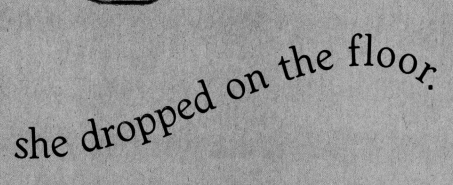

she dropped on the floor.

Then I'll nap on her bed
and have a good snore.

What's that? WOOF!
Could it be her car door?

"I'm home!" she called.
"I've been to the store."

"There's something for you.
Come over here, please.

Have a carrot,

some broccoli,

some squash,

a few peas."

"No peas?" said my mistress.
"I should have known."
Then she reached in a bag . . .

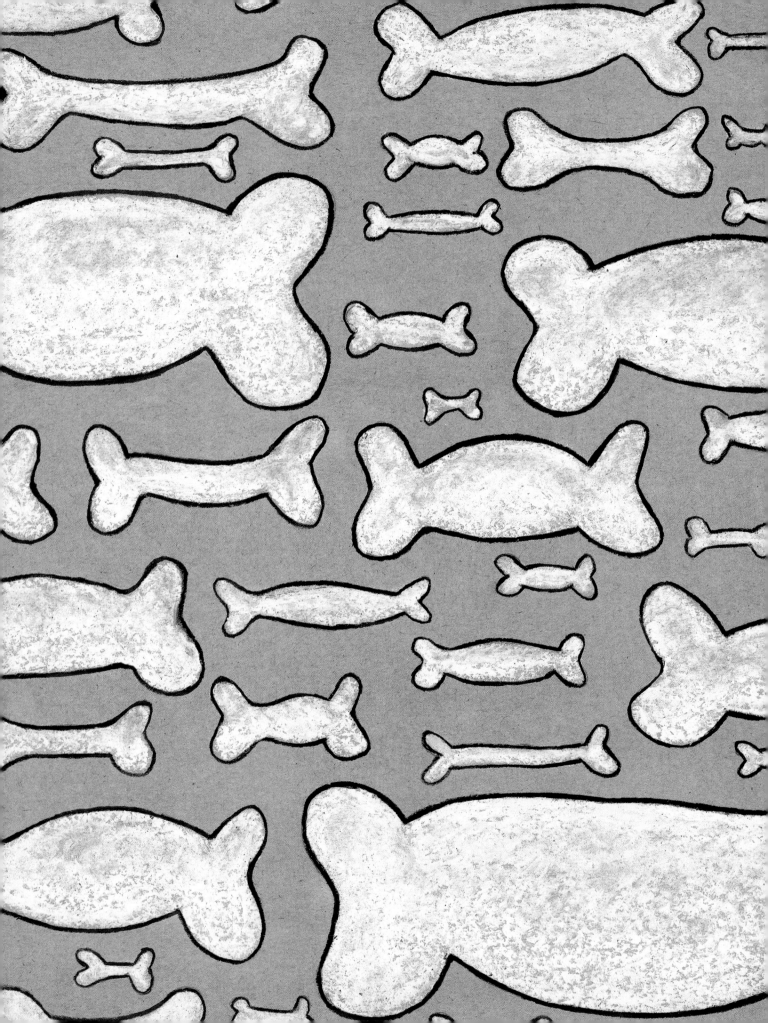

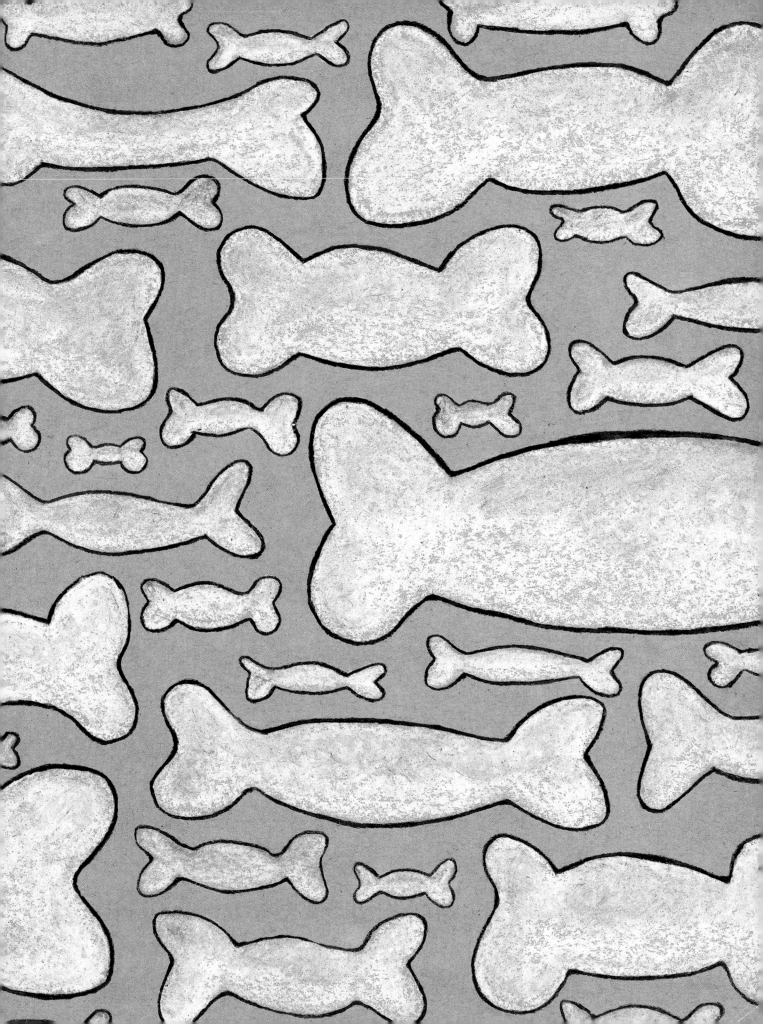